Ladybird I'm Ready... for Phonics!

Note to parents, carers and teachers

Ladybird I'm Ready for Phonics is a series of phonic reading books that have been carefully written to give gradual, structured practice of the synthetic phonics programme your child is learning at school.

Each book focuses on a set of phonemes (sounds) together with their graphemes (letters). The books also provide practice of common tricky words, such as **the** and **said**, that cannot be sounded out.

The series closely follows the order that your child is taught phonics in school, from initial letter sounds to key phonemes and beyond. It helps to build reading confidence through practice of these phonics building blocks, and reinforces school learning in a fun way.

Ideas for use

- Children learn best when reading is a fun experience. Read the book together and give your child plenty of praise and encouragement.

- Help your child identify and sound out the phonemes (sounds) in any words she is having difficulty reading. Then, blend these sounds together to read the word.

- Talk about the story words, high-frequency words and tricky words at the end of the stories to reinforce learning.

For more information and advice on synthetic phonics and school book banding, visit **www.ladybird.com/phonics**

Book Band 1

Level 3 builds on the sounds learnt in levels 1 and 2
and introduces new sounds and their letter representations:

m   d   o   g   c   k   ck

Special features:

repetition of sounds
in different words

short sentences with
simple language

Top Dog nods and
Sam Cat sits in it.

Can I
sit in it?

Pompom

8

9

Story Words

Can you match these words to the
pictures below?

Top Dog

Pompom

Sam Cat

Tom Ant

Tim Kid

16

Tricky Words

These tricky words are in the story
you have just read. They cannot
be phonetically sounded out. Can
you memorize them and read them
super fast?

I
into
go
no

17

summary page to
reinforce learning

Written by Monica Hughes
Illustrated by Chris Jevons

Phonics and Book Banding Consultant: Kate Ruttle

A catalogue record for this book is available from the British Library

Published by Ladybird Books Ltd
80 Strand, London, WC2R 0RL
A Penguin Company

001

ISBN: 978-0-72327-539-8
Printed in China

Ladybird I'm Ready... for Phonics!

Top Dog and Pompom

Top Dog got into Pompom.

7

Top Dog nods and Sam Cat sits in it.

Pompom

Top Dog nods and
Tom Ant sits in it.

10

Pompom dips as
Tim Kid sits in it.

Tim Kid panics and kicks Sam Cat.

Tom Ant panics and nips Top Dog.

Pompom tips!

Story Words

Can you match these words to the pictures below?

Top Dog

Pompom

Sam Cat

Tom Ant

Tim Kid

Tricky Words

These tricky words are in the story you have just read. They cannot be phonetically sounded out. Can you memorize them and read them super fast?

I

into

go

no

Ladybird I'm Ready... for Phonics!

Top Dog is Sick

Top Dog can not dig.
Top Dog is sick.

21

Top Dog naps.
Top Dog is sick
and Sam Cat is sad.

Sam Cat got Doc Panda.

Tim Kid and Tom Ant got Top Dog socks.

Top Dog picks a comic.
Top Dog sits.

Top Dog is not sick.
Top Dog can dig.

29

Story Words

Can you match these words to the pictures below?

Top Dog

Doc Panda

Sam Cat

Tom Ant

Tim Kid

socks

comic

High-frequency Words

These high-frequency (common) words are in the story you have just read. Can you read them super fast?

a

can

not

is

and

got

on

Collect all
Ladybird I'm Ready... for Phonics!

Captain Comet's Space Party

9780723275374

Nat Naps!

9780723275381

Top Dog

9780723275398

Huff! Puff! Run!

9780723275404

Fix It Vets

9780723275411

Dash is Fab!

9780723275428

Say the Sounds

9780723271598

Flashcards

9780723272069

Ladybird I'm Ready for... apps are now available for iPad, iPhone and iPod touch.

Apps also available on Android devices